**FRIENDS
OF ACPL**

My Friend Charlie

Story and Pictures by JAMES FLORA

ME

←CHARLIE

HARCOURT, BRACE & WORLD, INC.

NEW YORK

Other Books by James Flora

THE FABULOUS FIREWORK FAMILY
THE DAY THE COW SNEEZED
CHARLIE YUP AND HIS SNIP-SNAP BOYS
LEOPOLD, THE SEE-THROUGH CRUMBPICKER
KANGAROO FOR CHRISTMAS

FOR JOHN CYRUS,
DON AND PAUL

CONTENTS

WHY I LIKE CHARLIE

My friend Charlie is a pretty good old friend. I couldn't like him any better than I do, even if he owned a pony and an air rifle.

There are lots of reasons why I like Charlie.

Here are some:

1. He gives me half of whatever he is eating.
2. Sometimes he lets me be the pitcher in the ball game, even though he owns the ball.
3. Charlie never laughs at my nose.
4. Sometimes when I am about to be eaten by dragons, Charlie saves me.
5. Once when I cut my hand, Charlie cried too.

And another good reason is that Charlie can think of lots of good things to do. Let me tell you about some of them.

CHARLIE
SAVES A CAT

Cats like to climb up trees, but they sure hate to climb down. Some cats will sit up in a tree all day and cry until someone comes to help them down. Most people don't help cats in trees. They call the fire department. But my friend Charlie always helps cats.

One day Charlie heard a "miaow" up in a tree. That was the day he invented a new way to get cats out of trees.

He went home and got a bucket and a rope and a fish. He put the fish in the bucket and tied one end of the rope to the handle. He threw

the other end of the rope over a limb up above
the cat and pulled up the bucket.

The cat smelled the fish and jumped into the
bucket, and Charlie brought the bucket down.

That cat had an elevator ride and a fish dinner
all at the same time. She liked it. Now she won't
leave Charlie, follows him everywhere. Charlie
says she just wants more fish, but I think she
really likes Charlie just as I do.

CHARLIE GETS SWALLOWED BY A GOAT

harlie and I were walking on Mrs. Murphy's fence. Mrs. Murphy's goat came up and started to nibble on Charlie's shoes.

"That goat is always trying to eat me," he said. "Today I think I'll let him."

"Don't do that, Charlie," I begged him. "You're my best friend, and I wouldn't want you to get hurt inside a goat."

"Pooh!" he said. "I'm going to let that old goat swal-

low me, and it won't hurt a bit."

He pulled a photograph of himself out of his pocket. He piled some grass on top of it and gave it to the goat. The goat ate it with one gulp.

"See!" Charlie laughed and laughed. "I told you it wouldn't hurt to be swallowed by that goat."

It was such a goofy joke that I chased Charlie all the way home and rubbed dandelions on his nose.

I wish I could think of good jokes the way Charlie does.

CHARLIE BORROWS MY DREAM

"I had a good dream last night," I told Charlie. "I dreamed that I had a two-wheeler bicycle that could go anywhere. I rode it right up one side of a tree and down the other. I rode it up and down all the houses on the way to school. When I got to school, I rode all over the ceiling and sideways across the blackboard. Teacher was surprised."

"Say! That's a real whizzer of a dream," Charlie said. "Let me borrow that dream tonight. Will you? I'll let you dream my

rocket-to-the-moon dream. It's a good one, too."

"Sure, Charlie," I said. "You can borrow it tonight."

The next day Charlie said, "I sure do like that old bicycle dream of yours. I'm going to keep it a few more nights and add some nice parts to it."

Charlie dreamed my dream for a whole week, and when he gave it back, it was much better. It had new parts in it where I ride the bicycle over mountains and tugboats and under the ocean and over whales and right into the White House in Washington. Then the President of the United States says to me, "You are, without doubt, the very best bicycle rider in the whole world," and he shakes my hand and pins a medal on me.

You can always tell when somebody is your friend. When he borrows a dream, he always takes good care of it and fixes it up better than ever before he gives it back.

CHARLIE MAKES A HORSE LAUGH

Charlie and I were coming home from school one day when we saw this sad horse. It was hitched to a milk wagon.

"That poor horse needs a good laugh," Charlie said. "I think I'll tell him a joke."

Charlie went right up and started to whisper in the sad horse's ear. In no time at all that horse started to giggle and laugh.

"HA-HA! HO-HO! HEE-HEE!" You know how horses laugh.

"What joke did you tell that horse?" I asked Charlie.

"I told him some horse jokes," Charlie said. "I thought he would like horse jokes best. First I told him about the horse who came to a big river. He asked a duck, 'Can I walk across here?'

" 'Oh, yes!' said the duck. 'It's very shallow.'

"The horse walked into the river, but soon he was in over his head. He had to swim all the way to the other side. 'I

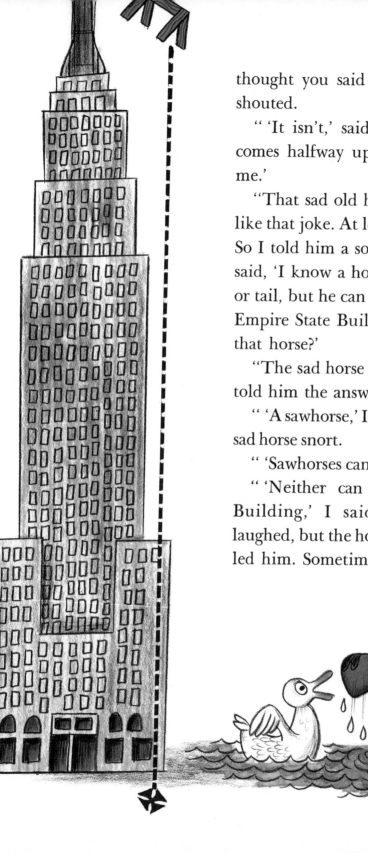

thought you said it wasn't deep,' he shouted.

" 'It isn't,' said the duck. 'It only comes halfway up on my father and me.'

"That sad old horse didn't seem to like that joke. At least he didn't laugh. So I told him a sort of horse riddle. I said, 'I know a horse that has no eyes or tail, but he can jump as high as the Empire State Building. Do you know that horse?'

"The sad horse shook his head, so I told him the answer.

" 'A sawhorse,' I said. That made the sad horse snort.

" 'Sawhorses can't jump,' he said.

" 'Neither can the Empire State Building,' I said. I laughed and laughed, but the horse didn't, so I tickled him. Sometimes you find a horse with no sense of humor, and tickling is the only way you can get him to laugh."

"Hold on there, Charlie," I called. "You just said that sad horse answered you. You know very well that horses can't talk."

Charlie giggled and jumped over a fence. I chased him, just as I always do, but I can never catch Charlie. He's too fast.

But do you know, that horse was still laughing the next morning when he delivered the milk to our house. Maybe he really did like Charlie's jokes.

I did. Did you?

CHARLIE TALKS TO FISH

I went swimming with Charlie one day. He carried a long piece of pipe. I said, "What's that, Charlie? A bean shooter?"

"No siree," said Charlie. "That's my fish phone. I always talk to fish before I swim."

"HOO-HA-HA!" I had to laugh. "You're crazy, Charlie. People can't talk to fish. Everybody knows that."

Charlie didn't say anything. When we got to the pond, he put one end of his fish phone in the water and shouted into the other.

"ELMER! HEY, ELMER!" Charlie yelled. "ARE THERE ANY TUR-

TLES OR BROKEN BOTTLES DOWN THERE?"

As soon as he had shouted, Charlie put his ear to the fish phone. He must have heard something because his eyes opened up wide.

"You don't say? Is that a fact? Hmmm-m-m. Now isn't that terrible! Yes. I'll tell him."

Charlie turned to me. He looked very sad.

"Now you've gone and done it," he said. "Elmer says that a big submarine down there is stuck in the bubble gum you lost yesterday when you made that big belly whopper. They want you to come down right away and get your bubble gum so everybody on the submarine can get home in time for dinner."

It was such a goofy joke that I chased Charlie. He slipped in the mud and made a big belly whopper just as I did yesterday.

Charlie is so goofy! He's just like me, only more. That's why I like to swim with Charlie.

CHARLIE POLISHES A PIG AND WINS A PRIZE

Charlie was going to take his pig, Charlotte, to the fair. He said she would win a prize, and we could eat ice-cream cones with the money. I helped him wash Charlotte and tie a pink ribbon on her tail. Charlie looked her over.

"She still looks kind of scruffy," he said. "Like an old shoe that's been out in the rain all night." I could see an idea pop into his head because his ears always rattle around when he thinks of something.

He went into the house and came out with some polish and a brush. We polished Charlotte until she sparkled like a new Ford car. She was so proud! She kept looking around at herself, the way girls in new dresses do.

She won the prize all right, just as Charlie said, and we ate ice-cream cones until our toes got cold.

The only trouble is that now we have to polish Charlotte every day. She gets sad and sorrowful if we don't. And that's a lot of work polishing a whole pig, as you well know if you have ever polished one. But I always help Charlie. That's what friends are for—to help each other with all of the polishing and things.

CAN YOU SKATE ON YOUR HEAD AND EAT NOODLES LIKE CHARLIE?

"Do you know what I can do?" Charlie asked one morning in July. "I can skate on my head."

"Pooh," I said. "Nobody but circus people can skate on their heads."

But Charlie did. He buckled a skate on his head, and sure enough, he rolled down the sidewalk upside down. He could go around in circles too.

"I can do even more," Charlie bragged. "I can eat noodles upside down too."

He went inside his house and got a plate of noodles and a knife and fork and napkin. He skated around on his head while he ate all the noodles. Then he wiped his mouth with his napkin. It was a beautiful sight to see.

I know people who are very good at athletics like skating. And I know people who are very good at eating. But my friend Charlie is the only one I know who can do both, upside down, and mind his table manners at the same time.

EATING PEANUTS
WITH YOUR FOOT

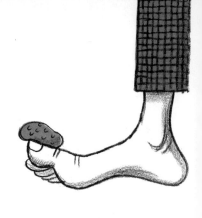

"Can you eat peanuts with your foot?" Charlie asked.

I said, "I don't know, but I'll try. Wait'll I get my shoe off."

"No, no," Charlie said. "You have to do it with your shoes on."

Well, I tried and tried, but I couldn't do it. Finally I

said, "I'll bet four rides on my scooter that you can't do it either."

Charlie just smiled. He took a board and laid it over a rock like a teeter-totter. He put a peanut on one end and stamped his foot on the other. The peanut flew through the air and plopped right into Charlie's mouth.

That's another thing I like about Charlie—every day you learn something new and important from him.

CHARLIE GETS A LETTER FROM THE MOON ⭐

"I got a letter from the moon today," Charlie said. "Do you want to know what it says?"

"Sure," I said. "I never heard from the moon in my whole life."

"It says, 'Dear Charlie: I saw you the other night when you stayed up until ten-thirty playing hide-and-seek. That is too late, and your mother was worried. I hope you won't do that again.

'And why do you keep telling people that I am made of green cheese when you know very well that I'm made of rocks? Please tell the truth about me.

'Thanks for sending me all the doughnuts and gum-drops last week. They were very good. I don't get much good food up here except when some kind friend remembers to send me some.

'Can you come up here for a visit next week? It would be nice to have you. Bring your pajamas, and you can bring your friend George if you like.

Sincerely,

your friend The Moon

'P.S. Please bring some new flashlight batteries when you come. I think mine are wearing out. I don't seem to shine as brightly as I did last year.'"

"That's goofy," I said. "How can you go to the moon?

How can the moon eat gumdrops? And you know very
well he doesn't need batteries to shine. Where did you
get that crazy letter, Charlie?"

"I made it up," said Charlie. "I always wanted a letter
from the moon, but I never got one until today. I think
I'll go. Do you want to go along?"

We went and had a wonderful time. Just make believe,
of course.

THINGS NOT TO DO

"I'm making a list of things not to do!" Charlie was writing on paper. "It will help me stay out of trouble. Whenever I think of something I want to do, I'll just look and see if it is on this list. If it is, I won't do it."

"I'll help you," I said. "I know lots of things not to do."

Here is the THINGS NOT TO DO list that we made. You can use it if you want. It sure makes life a lot easier for Charlie and me. Maybe it will do the same for you.

DON'T TIE KNOTS IN SNAKES

DON'T STEP ON PIGS UNLESS YOU ARE BAREFOOT

DON'T EAT THE BOTTOMS OF ICE-CREAM CONES BEFORE YOU EAT THE TOPS

DON'T PUT WORMS IN YOUR FATHER'S SHOES

DON'T PUT PEANUT BUTTER ON HORSES OR TURTLES

DON'T PAINT YOUR HEAD RED

DON'T DREAM ABOUT MONSTERS

DON'T TRADE YOUR MOTHER TO GYPSIES

DON'T GIVE BUBBLE GUM TO FISH

DON'T SIT ON CROCODILES

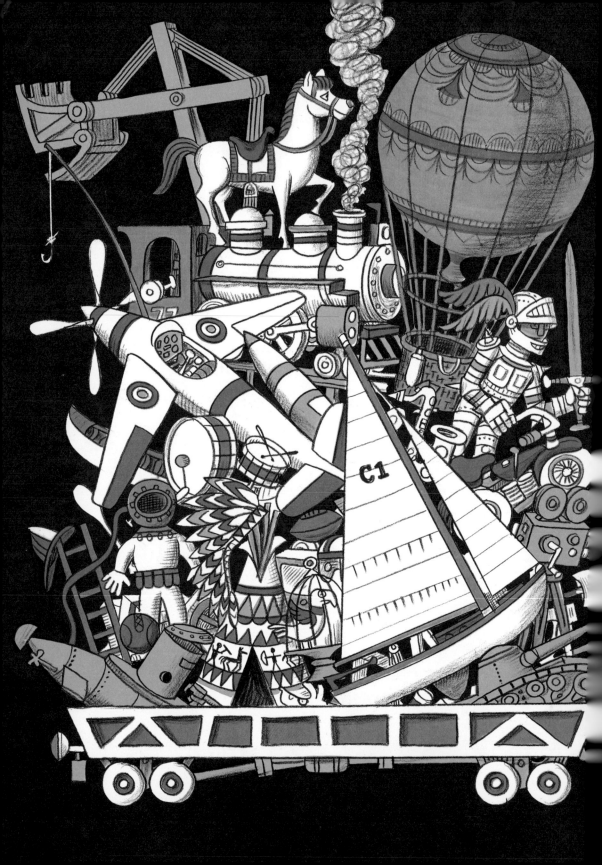

A PICTURE OF ALL THE THINGS I AM GOING TO GIVE TO CHARLIE

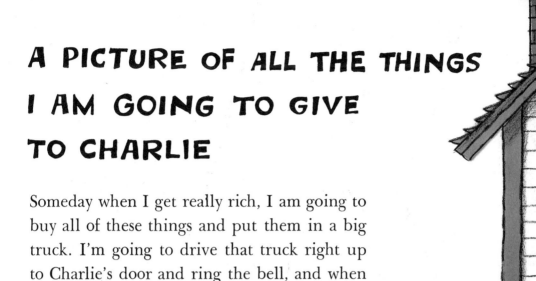

Someday when I get really rich, I am going to buy all of these things and put them in a big truck. I'm going to drive that truck right up to Charlie's door and ring the bell, and when he comes out, I'm going to say, "Here, Charlie. These things are for you, because anybody as nice as you should have had them a long time ago."

That should make Charlie happy. Then we can play with them together. I know Charlie will let me.

Best friends always do.